Dedicated to David Unaipon
(Aboriginal man on Australia's $50 banknote.)

Australia's first Aboriginal English-writing story-teller
and our own – and only – 'Da-Vinci'

THE FETHAFOOT CHRONICLES

CONTENTS

THE FETHAFOOT CHRONICLES

Within the following Chronicles survive the rich, untold stories of the enigmatic *Fethafoot* Clan. These are tales from Australia's ancient first people and their beloved sacred land, which they called, Heart-rock: that mysterious sunburnt, harsh terrain of ever-changing ecosystems, commonly known worldwide as *The Land Down Under*. On the following pages you will find a number of the oral accounts of those feared shaman, witch doctors or evil spirits also known individually as the *Kadaicha-man*.

These chronicles will quench the thirsty query into that extensive, intriguing disparity of times between the Aboriginal Dreamtime – when the Creation Spirits roamed the flat dead skin of our land – to when the pale-skinned Ghost-people began their hungry quest across *The Mother's* skin and down through the decades until contemporary times.

When the land-thirsty *Ghosts* finally reached Australia just a few short generations ago, they found a society of inhabitants that had grown to almost a million souls and had adapted to and were thriving in this harsh land's unforgiving conditions. They found them thriving over every single portion of the great southern land. However, as for knowledge of my clan, they heard only whispers of supernatural myth and legend – and that, only after discovering that my people spoke as many languages as there were boundaries of the six-hundred plus extended families who each cared for their own nation states – with an intense passion, as profound as the divine passions that had driven the Ghost's own sacred beliefs and terrible conflicts. As with the Australian Aborigine, Bidjigal warrior *Pemulwuy* – who led the coastal *Eora* people's fight for survival and remarkably prevailed against the first strange, pale-skinned invaders of his people's lands for 12 harsh years – my own clan name and the mysteries surrounding it have been removed from public knowledge and history, until now.

Such secrecy is not perceived as a negative for our clan. It is what we have continuously desired. To perform the type of work we are engaged in, secrecy or concealment of our clan is a prerequisite to safeguard our small and utterly loyal family and its works from public knowledge …

THE AUTHOR

I am what some in the clan would call most favoured – certainly, honoured. This is not because my work is any easier than my ancient or recent predecessors; rather, it is said because I now have the power – via the written word and an eager knowledge of such descriptive, written language – to ensure that our deeds are remembered in our land, and not just by the clan and those in need of our help.

For the first time in our known history, we have a way to reveal the long and intriguing history of our clan to the *Johnny-come-lately* Ghost People's descendants – and the many new peoples who now also call this majestic, sacred land home.

Whether indigenous or non, if you were born in Australia – or Heart-rock Land – you may have heard of mythical tales of some of our warriors' often disconcerting manifestations. These are dusty old tales kept in great-grandfather's cupboard and only dragged out on eerie, windswept nights and even then, only whispered about around flittering campfires and close family gatherings. Spine-tingling tales about the mysterious, often terrifying, Australian Aboriginal magic-man, or *Kadaicha-man* as our clan-family of warriors were to become known as, by our own people in the beginning …

THE CLAN

Listen! Heart-rock people! The infamous Fethafoot are still at work today, upholding the law and standards given by the Dreaming ancestors to maintain the links between the heavens, the land and its creatures, in a stable and *essential* balance.

It has been passed down that the Fethafoot family and its covert work began not long after the start of time, as we know it, in *The Mother's Dreaming time*, after the Dreamtime creation spirits established order. It was a time when one of the creations – that one given language – began to consider itself as superior to all other creatures. These rather wonderful creatures quickly became proud and selfish, insular and arrogant; soon even forgetting why they were bequeathed their part in the cycle of time on The Mother incarnate. Aghast at the pride and irreverence displayed by the air, fire, earth and water language-creatures – so we are told – the ancient elders decided that another separate clan was required – a force to match the singular self-centredness that was swiftly overtaking the lives and pathways of their final beautiful creations.

Our stories utter that these moulded, walking talking wonders were formed especially to maintain the proper balance between the Earth Mother and the Sky Spirit's heavens, but alas, they buried that knowledge under self-centred admiration and self-importance, even before the last Dreamtime Spirit's glorious rumblings of creation had faded. Thus, the Fethafoot Clan was created. Fethafoot men and women were warrior trained to support the Dreamtime design: to guide the people along the proper path so the cycle of life between the people animals land and their mutual connections with the Dreaming would stay wholesome, mutually nourishing – unbroken.

Initially, clan warriors were only amply trained in the usual skills that our people needed to survive: basic weaponry, spying, hand-to-hand combat and the like. However, the clan was nothing if not open-minded, hungry for knowledge, and long-term future oriented. Soon the clan began to seek, analyse and utilise any and all martial art, magic, weaponry or mind-training skills that we heard about, or encountered. Consequently, very early on in the clan's growth, our elders began to train our young warriors in mental, physical and spiritual abilities. Spiritually, often in somewhat dangerous areas of powerful magic – unknown to most and never heard of at all – by the narcissistic majority.

We learned about and were trained from youth, in numerous one-on-one fighting skills. Many of these styles were acquired from supple, agile, athletic warriors that came from our northern neighbours across the Mother's liquid skin. We'd learnt that these calm, confident, well-balanced, short men could do unheard of feats of combat forms and the clan invited them to our own great gatherings, where such fighting styles could be tried out against a real opponent. We found too that these warriors had learned such over many generations and from many nations all across their own great lands, which they alleged to be as large as the clan's beloved Heart-rock land.

We learned skills that reinforced and added to our own practical, innate and invented forms of combat and information gathering. And, from the very beginning, we were taught that the value of reputation was as strong a force as any actual incredible feat. It was drummed into each young initiate that force is not always the best option in any solution and that wisdom time and thought will surely gain better outcomes than emotional or over-enthusiastic instant reaction. We were taught how to exercise the mind and improve the mental abilities of memory, total awareness and forethought planning.

The early years of training – when a child's mind is most unfortified to the fantastic, or the implausible – focused heavily on practising the mental skills of Heart-rock's dark-skinned dugong eating northern islanders, whose magical-mental abilities have been written about as *The Drums of Mer*, in which certain Torres Strait Island *clever-men* sent messages of warning and of plentiful foods via a trained and focused powerful sixth sense, and over great distances between their island homes. Thus, the clan have utilised and adapted even this unique gift to develop mind-joining abilities with our totem animals that allowed trained warriors to see with the animal's eyes and hear with their astute ears …

THE CHRONICLES

During the following chronicles – in each tale passed down orally by our clan over many, many generations – you will find that some of our warriors were radically advanced in a form of spiritual Dreaming-travel. Hence, they did not always travel via foot – *in the flesh*, via 'foot-walking' or *"Shanks Pony"*, as walking is often called in 'Auss' – as do normal people. These warriors use the *Dreaming lines* that the creation beings left behind, to move across the land as needed. These lines of Dreamtime power run still, all across our beloved lands. Thus, we became known as The Fethafoot: an ancient mystery – unknown even whether we were one or many – though always fear-provoking beings that could come and go at will, leaving no trace: spirit-warriors that accomplished exceptional solutions to complex conundrums, often with the use of magical powers and were thought by the many to be spirits, rather than men of flesh and blood.

One of our most profound weapons ever created against the shameless – those corrupted language-creatures that our clan dealt with – and, that we knew worked extremely well from practical experience – was that the clan trained women as well as men to fully initiated warrior status. From svelte and vibrant youthful beauties, to wiry mothers and on to old wrinkled white-hairs who were never thought to be anything but mundane tribal women and as such, thought of by most males especially, as the more *naïve* of the genders. But who were in fact, extremely deadly warrior-women who could watch, listen and act totally innocently and, according to our particular needs.

We are taught that equality between men and women was what our Dreaming ancestors created; each aspect of the male and female language-creature made to complement the other. This gender-impartial Dreaming decree, – as is all Fethafoot law – has been lost and then returned to the Heart-rock people many, many times throughout our known history according to our own legends. Thus, to our belief and experience, adherence to the law has gained our primary function an almost invisible weapon and revealed our warrior women to be as robust, intelligent and cunning as any other warrior among our deadly family clan. This tenet and subsequent behaviour of course, led to the women in our clandestine extended family to soon become the initial women's libbers of our country, and woe-betide the warrior who felt that *they* were lower than men in the grand scheme!

FETHAFOOT HISTORY

The known, recognised evidence of the history and archaeology of our common world speaks of great floods, of creeping movements of the great continents, of massive volcanoes and the deaths of whole species over millions of years.

Our own oral history speaks of six cataclysms: six *lifting* of the Mother's veils that scoured the Mother's surface clean, with the final apocalyptic event occurring around the time that archaeologists found evidence of our people's first campfires and long-lived remains. Our history talks of six periods of time before such records as Mungo man and various cave drawings that dated our ancestors. It speaks of times of prolonged unrelenting changes, when the Mother wrestled passionately within herself. For our people, these were an unforgiving, harsh epoch of times that taught our people the necessity of fast, practical adaptation. Seeing firsthand what happened to extinct animals that did not heed the Mother's all-encompassing lesson: *adapt quickly or disappear utterly*, the people of Heart-rock looked and *saw*, listened, *heard* and acted.

Listen well reader: the Fethafoot clan right across our Heart-rock land – from east to west and top to bottom – laughed out long and hard when Captain Cook's Ghost-people arrived here, and quickly began to believe that our people would wink out of existence, solely because of their arrival. The phrase, Buryl-dandji-Gneemull (alike to What The!), was exclaimed more than once or twice around Fethafoot fires at this ill-informed prediction ...

A HARDY PEOPLE

Why the laughter you ask? Our people have survived through one hundred year droughts, when freshwater was so scarce for so long that some of the fearful and ignorant in our society, began to worship *that* liquid gift. Sadly, Fethafoot warriors had to despatch several shameless stubborn hard-heads, to stop that corruption from entering our society. When ice and snow covered almost every part of our land and large terrifying air and water breathing carnivores found our people to be easier prey than the diverse, often violently opposed to becoming food creatures that roamed the Mother, it was Fethafoot who worked out ways and means of killing and capturing the things – and bringing to an end the ignorant rituals of many fearful, superstitious tribes; several of whom had begun sacrificing their own clans-people to the great hungry beasts.

Yet again, when great rocks, hot dust and fire rained down from the sky, bringing darkness and biting ash that laid thickly on the ground and killed everything it touched. When the Mother's skin erupted from her own great bursts of uncontrollable energy. When her molten blood exploded upward and ran across our lands from deep down in her broiling gut, it was the clan who found safe caves, fissures, shelter, safe places under protection. And it was Fethafoot who then adapted the people's food and drinking sources to survive, until the smoke and ash cleared away – some generations later.

Let it be well known that this brief clash of cultures will *not* destroy us; we are strong, quick to adapt and eager to learn. That's how we have survived so well for so long – and all in isolation from the rest of the world's knowledge in this harsh, ever-changing land.

Note well, dear reader that as far as our oral records inform, the Heart-rock people learned very early not to lust after another's home, lands, or anything else not ceded by the law to us at birth. The earth, all waters and this majestic land is ceded to us as *caretakers* – never *owners*. Yes, today we too may *buy* land, but if you see and grasp the notion of the holistic Dreaming life, you will know that one can never own even the tiniest part of any actual living entity, which the Mother is. As real and as alive as the very atoms of which we find that we are composed. *She* is a very, very big living atom.

My clan's fondest wish today is that we – black, brown, white, yellow and all shades between – Australians, turn as a nation and look to my people's past. Look and *see*.

The way we are using the Mother today, we will be lucky to see another 500 years and yet my people lived generation after generation, after generation within *Her* parameters. We don't have to drop the electric light, but we must fight for her welfare. In the short run of each of our lives, it is not just our own future we gamble with, but The Mother's hope as well …

A 'PALE' JOKE

Allow me to depart from this edifying excursion for a moment to let you in on a historical joke in respect to the many, many years of name-calling, slander and calumniation that has always been a part of any historical clash of cultures. It seems that Pemulwuy and his 'clever-man' peers were so intensely shocked at the white-skinned people's lack of understanding of spiritualty and knowledge; of that balance between the heavens and the earth – that the only way they had of describing such, was to use their language-name for a fat white grub, whose lazy life-cycle allowed them to be harvested easily and frequently.

Recently, when our people first heard the name that contemporary Australians had given to the large, beautiful white whales that swim up and down our coastlines annually, it almost caused death-by-laughter among some of our people. The name Miglo, or Migaloo, used so gleefully by TV newsreaders everywhere, also happened to be the expression used for those first Ghost invaders, and not for any physical features, apart from their pale colouring, but for the seemingly total blind ignorance of any genuine knowledge of what *they* saw as *any* genuine spirituality. Thus, the word Miglo was often used in the same context as non-indigenous folk used the words Abo, coon, boong, nigger, gin and other derogatory names that have been used to describe our people. Today, our people use this name as a descriptive more than a judgmental term, although every time those magnificent creatures arrive on our coasts, it is not unusual to see an elder white-hair Aborigine still cackling and tickled pink at that name's relished and widespread use …

A CUSTOMARY WELCOME

This trifling amount of information should give you some idea of the Fethafoot and some of their abilities. You will discover more as you read the various chronicles and, as the need for our hard earned various skills occur throughout the accounts.

Today, wherever you are on the great blessed Mother's skin – the joining place between our world and the heavens – it's now time to snuggle up in a favourite spot with the Mothers' and the Great Spirit's corporeal forms' touching you, to give the life-giving fresh air and perhaps if we are lucky, some of heaven's warm life-giving dappled sunshine. Sit back comfortably there and utilise the fantastic gift that the pale-skinned Ghost-people brought to our land – the written word and the ability to decipher and understand such – which may be a small thing to the pale-skinned Ghosts, but an enormous and wonderful gift to the knowledge-hungry Fethafoot. Please – enjoy my wonderful adaptive, indomitable, Australian Aboriginal people's delight in the ability to tell our stories for the first time since our colourful, eventful, magical Dreaming lives began: perhaps even as far back as 100,000 years ago.

The following chronicles are true and although not in any chronological order, they have been faithfully recorded just as they were handed down; and now, with the three R's of *ritin, readin an rithmatic* being commonplace among my people, they are available for all Australians to enjoy and to sample the mostly unknown treasures of your ancient people's vibrant past. The stories will also reveal the largely unheard of moral and ethical heart of my people, from Dreamtime to contemporary times in our exciting, continuously changing wonderful part of the Mother that we believe we were made caretakers of; until *She* too, will pass …

NYARLA AND THE CIRCLE OF STONES

PROLOGUE

As told to me by my mother Nuutchuus, who was told by her father's father, Bitchun-goori, who was told by his mother, Narindoo, and on back and into the obscure past; a tale about a particular task, which the Fethafoot were engaged to solve about 13 generations past …

Nigh on 650 years ago, in the centre of the land now called Australia, the environment, including weather and plant life was very different from what we see now. Although food and water were not as plentiful out there as they were on and near our coastlines, times were good for the *Carers* of the area in which this story unfolded. At that time, elder Fethafoot were living with the Gungurri people, near what is presently known as Charleville, in southern Queensland: land that was known only as Gungurri land then. Our clan had been asked to that Dreaming land to mediate between two Gungurri groups, who had an ongoing water dispute issue that had gotten totally out of hand.

Several of the young men on both sides of the dispute had fought battles over the water rights, and the argument had become much more serious, in that one group had called in an immoral Clever-man, who had immediately begun to *Sing* an up and coming young warrior from the opposing group. Elders from both tribes now felt that the conflict had gone too far and their own attempts to solve the issue had failed badly, resulting in a loss of face for these esteemed elder group from both factions. A few minor skirmishes and a fight-challenge were okay, the local elders believed, but playing with a legitimately merciless solution was playing with fire, and usually, everyone involved got burned in some way; a fact they knew from harsh experience.

However, that particular affair was easily solved and took only a few sore heads and even fewer moons to solve, although *that* particular tale is for another night's telling, around another campfire altogether …

Eerwa: the Terror

At about that time – as it has been for all time in our long journey throughout this land – there were consistent travelling storytellers; keen listeners, gaining knowledge and tales to spread exciting new stories and information all around our country, wherever they travelled. These story-gatherers followed well-worn, permanent trading paths that cut across tribal boundaries – rivers, deserts and clan lands. However, one bloodcurdling tale in particular continued to rise up its ugly head from the morass of other stories, news and rumour.

This tale voiced dark whispers about a terrible, evil spirit-man who was killing and "disappearing" men and women in the desert, near the centre of our land, around the great red heart-rock of our land's naming – Uluru – the Heart-rock itself ...

CHAPTER 1

CENTRAL AUSTRALIA, 1360, NEAR ULURU:

[NB: about the same time that the Jewish story of Joshua at Jericho was said to be occurring in the Middle East]

The cunning night-coated predator moved like a wraith, flowing across the ground and through the landscape rather than needing to walk across and on it, and thus, leaving no tell-tale marks that a tracker or hunter could follow. His prey – a thin, wiry young man yet a half a kilometre away – abruptly sensed something brush past and both his body and young naive spirit shivered involuntarily. The young man literally shook it off, preferring to believe that it was the cool of early morning that caused the subconscious shudder. Besides, *he* was a recently welcomed full warrior of his tribe and he could show or reveal no fear, especially to his most recent peers who would soon join him.

It was still dark now, just before the false dawn, though the young man was ready and rearing for the early start of a hunt with several important men from his clan's tribe. The camp nearby was quiet, with mothers and infants alike finally dropping into deep sleep for a few blissful hours in that quiet stillness preceding the true dawn, before the light and heat wake them for another day. There was no time for goodbyes or food this morning; just time to grab his best weapons and some dried food, which he had prepared days ago and now carried in a skin and twine bag around his waist. He was excited and anxious, though suitably prepared for this hunt and now he waited patiently, quietly, at the appointed meeting place for the other hunters to arrive.

He was early, but he'd been extra keen for this hunt and as he waited near a small billabong, he knelt down to the water at the sloping bank, dropping his head down to quench his night's thirst. He held himself from the water with his strong arms and shoulders, hands flat right at the edge of the water as he sucked the cool water through his lips; even swallowing quietly as he would have to do very soon, when actually hunting. Noticing his own rippling reflection in the star-lit water, the young warrior thought again about the bleak, almost strangely ruthless, cold feeling he'd had just a short time ago. He gazed around nervously, but felt safe enough here, so close to his camp and brethren warriors. The other warriors would be here soon and then, no-one or nothing would stop them from carrying out their common obligation of providing food for the next few days for the clan elders. In the night's colourless tranquillity, as he took his fill from the still pool, the young man's thoughts quickly went back to the pride and respect he'd gain from this successful hunt.

Hearing a noise behind him, he began to rise to welcome his brother hunters, and if he had had the time, young Gilgardi would have screamed in fright. As he lifted his head from the wavering reflections of the starlit sky on the water, he saw a twisted rippling face appear on the water's surface above and behind him. Time seemed to stand still as he noticed the strange white criss-crossed face paint on the demonic face and noted the putrid smell that almost physically assaulted his nostrils, right down to his gut level, before he was hit on the back of his head and slumped into a swirling black, helpless unconsciousness …

A terrible nightmare

When he awoke sometime later, feeling as though he had been carried like a brained wallaby – woozy and painfully stiff – it was to moist, thick, creeping blackness: a black void and a cold vulnerable fear that he felt deep down to his core. It was like some instinctive ancient fear had been dredged up from some awful, gut-wrenching nightmare. Gilgardi knew immediately that he was not dead, because his head hurt like the devil where he'd been hit and he could feel the wetness of blood running down his neck and shoulders from the blow that had knocked him senseless. His eyes, ears and sense of smell strained to give him the data needed to gather his thoughts and actions, though the clasping blackness around him seemed solid, deadening – and his fearful trepidation consumed his blunted senses.

He soon discovered that he could smell and he earnestly wished that robust sense were dulled as well, because what he could smell was *death*. He tried to move and found that he was trussed up like a wallaby or emu that was to be kept alive: fattened and fresh for a Corroboree feast. Gilgardi had been a warrior and hunter for several years now, although only recently fully initiated and was not easily scared or frightened. He had, on many occasions laughed furtively at others who were proper-scared of being alone in the dark, or of the dreaded unseen magic men that all knew only lived for power over men and women and, who would do terrible deeds and acts to further that dark power. He also understood that if he gave in to panic now, he would exhaust himself and that would do nothing to help him get out of this terrible nightmare. Still, even now, he felt a small confidence that he had at least half a chance of escaping the fate that this evil spirit had planned for him, no matter how desperate the situation seemed right then. Gilgardi felt, rather than heard himself sigh and he wondered if the little grass-mouse felt the same misplaced confidence, as the eagle or kookaburra swooped down unseen from above.

That this was *the* bad spirit that had been whispered about for over 12 moons now, he had no doubt. Two travellers through the area had gone missing, only to turn up later dead and minus various body parts, though never before had anyone gone missing from a local major clan group. He and others in his clan had thought themselves exempt somehow from that terror. Now, as he came to consciousness, he was sure the same bad spirit had captured him and wanted his own still-living body parts for some hellish trickery or dark ceremony. Gilgardi groaned involuntarily in weak, helpless terror.

The smell in the dark cave or tunnel that he was in was simply overpowering. It cloyingly stuffed his other senses so full of death and decay that he could not seem to clear his sore head properly at all. He could not reason how long it had been since he was taken, or where he was, and that ever-present invasive, sour musky odour of death invaded every orifice and opening, overpowering all else. Unfortunately for Gilgardi's earnest and brave self-confidence and in fact his life, his abductor was presently watching him with glee, with the power of an absolute master over a slave shining out from his yellowed, sickly eyes. Whether he was man or spirit was difficult to determine, as he could not be discerned in the darkness. The fact that it had carried Gilgardi unconscious to this place, with seemingly little or no effort, leant toward it being of supernatural strength, if not supernatural origin, in Gilgardi's desperate, sense-starved mind.

The being watching Gilgardi actually respected the fact that this prey hadn't screamed or cried out, or wept, when it woke, and now it was hungry for the power that came from such a strong spirit. And in order to gather the power it needed from the sacred body parts, it next had to break poor Gilgardi's spirit by taking significant body parts needed for Gilgardi's continuing existence – but for its dark purposes, needed wet and pulsing and without the body that held them, to complete the next phase of its depraved scheme. These wet, bloody, sacred elements would be consumed by the dark magic to satisfy his craving for the corrupt power needed to gain full ascendancy over the small land area and people who lived there and that it already called its own.

Gilgardi was captive and bound tightly, in a cave deep in a naturally formed Mother's blood tunnel – a lava tube under a slight rocky ridgeline, only eight kilometres away from his family and home; though poor Gilgardi would never see his loved ones again in this dreaming cycle. At first he heard only whispers of movement and now and then a guttural, harsh voice speaking just loud enough to be heard. He couldn't understand the language and that in itself was startling, as he knew all the 20 or more languages used around this part of his beloved Heart-rock lands. Without warning, Gilgardi felt something live and rough touching him in the darkness, sliding lightly over the skin on his arm, then sliding across his face, onto his shoulders and down to his quivering shrivelled genitals.

When he bucked away from the slimy touch, Gilgardi realised that he was completely bound – and wholly naked. Although an extremely brave warrior, the darkness, his naked helplessness and the weird sounds echoing dully underground had by now totally unnerved him and he found himself mewling uncontrollably like a newborn babe – not yet able to speak language – except to whimper out that primal need of wanting comfort or sustenance. As his hope failed to find any spark and died, Gilgardi's deep shame spread out from his gut, carrying a terrible weakness to all his extremities.

Gilgardi had realised that he was in the middle of a cave or some type of large natural underground shelter. He could sense, feel and hear the evil thing whispering and touching itself and him as it moved a full turn around his bound body, its scratchy, dragging movements and predatory respiration bouncing back off the unseen walls and making it seem like there were sundry horrors surrounding him. After what seemed like hours of this draining torture, Gilgardi gave in to his terror. His bladder loosed uncontrollably and he urinated weakly, his hot urine steaming down his leg in the cool of the cave and against the heat of his fevered body. The bitter, tangy scent of it wafted strongly around him to remind him doubly of his helplessness and shame …

Eerwa

This was what the thing had awaited. Instantly, it moved behind Gilgardi, wrapped long hairy oiled arms around his body and with a flick of the wrist and a sharp stone knife, it took the full set of genitals from its prey. One moment, Gilgardi had one small memory of hope left – the next; a bright, stinging sensation later – he had pain, regret, defeat and sure death. He knew what the evil thing had taken and that he would die soon in its foul rotting lair; his own decaying body adding to the foulness clogging his mouth and nose.

Gilgardi accepted his coming passing, though with a deep, terrible sadness for his yet unlived life and he began to mumble out his just-learned, man's death song. However, even that small mercy was taken away, as the beast pulled his head back by his thick hair and used a small noose, fashioned from dried animal tendon to drop over and wrap around his tongue. Gilgardi felt rough, pungent, greasy fingers forced into his mouth to facilitate the noose's working. He groaned weakly, his voice choked off by the slip-noose around his tongue, while bleeding out from the wound at his groin. It grunted with satisfaction, stepped back a little, and then quickly, deftly, his tongue was pulled right out of his mouth, stretched painfully until it was out as far as it would go while he turned helplessly in his cocoon of bondage. Gilgardi could do nothing to stop it from happening as his life drained away. Again, it used the knife to cut out the instrument that gave flesh to language: an extremely valuable part of his dark quest.

Gilgardi could smell the scent of his own blood on the knife as it passed under his nose and took his tongue.

It now had the key pieces needed from this strong prey – the life-giver and its two seed carriers, as well as the instrument of language. All it needed now was the liver, the blood-cleanser of this brave warrior, who when faced with sure death had accepted his fate and begun his death song. The worst part for his victim was that it needed the final body-part for the ceremony from a living warrior. Although weak from blood loss and moving into the next life already, Gilgardi had one last gurgling scream of outrage left, as it speared the knife into his side and began to explore with a hairy brutal hand for the organ it needed.

As he went into deep shock and began to pass over, Gilgardi thought he heard it say its own name. Once – very quietly, though clearly – as if now that Gilgardi had given it his blood, flesh and tears: his very life forces, he could know *its* name. With no way to block his ears, the warrior heard it speak in his own language. "I am Eerwa: Serpent of Dread; *The* Terror," it hissed softly into his ear. "With your final gifts warrior, I will become all powerful," it said as Gilgardi gave up his spirit …

CHAPTER 2

SE QLD, 1360, GUNGURRI LAND

The Clan

It was after this disappearance that our clan-family was contacted by a "runner" named Buryl-danji, who had travelled by foot across the Arrernte, Wangkangurru, Karangura, Ngamini, Yawarawarka and Margany lands, to where the Gungurri mob were camped, to find the Fethafoot and seek our help. The recent disappearance of Gilgardi, a Pitjantjatara man who was related to a member of the Fethafoot family, had exposed such fear and terror that local warriors and medicine men in that area were being ridiculed by the seeming invincible ability of the bad spirit – to come and go as it pleased. It was also rumoured that this thing was gaining power and that all spiritual life in the area was at risk: meanwhile, *it* continued to grow stronger.

This disturbance of ritual maintenance for people and the land was very alarming for the people of the area around Heart-rock. The common spiritual life of the area sustained law, life and ceremonial maintenance to all the surrounding tribes. Thus, knowledge of creature movements, the health of waterholes and news from travellers in that large area of red, dry land stopped flowing, feeding fear and ignorance even further. All initiations had been stopped until the issue of the disappearances was resolved. Travel and the associated bartering that went hand in hand with that activity had stopped. Several small dangerous conflicts had begun. Young men and women did not attend their coming of age rituals as required and in their youthful exuberance took matters into their own hands, causing total mayhem in some cases …

The warrior is a woman!

Thus, at a Fethafoot meeting, the acknowledgement and importance of the events was agreed on and the family elders there, agreed to send a warrior back with the runner to confirm and perhaps deal with the issue. This was and is how the family conducted its business. A warrior is sent to confirm and then decide how best to solve the issue – and whether by themselves or with others of the clan. The chosen warrior in this case we are told was a young, exceptional woman. Her name was Nyarla and she was unquestionably of the Fethafoot blood and not an initiated member, as the family allowed entry to its ranks at various times. This *sending* revealed the Fethafoot's expressed wish for the problem to be solved quickly, although the runner Buryldanji was not to know that as yet. Nyarla and Buryldanji were cleansed by smoke and song for three full days, to fool the spirit or thing if it were that powerful, and to give health and strength to both warriors for a long speedy journey.

One moon's cycle after Gilgardi's disappearance near Uluru, Nyarla and Buryldanji began the long walk back to Buryldanji's home country of the Pitjantjatjara lands, near the great Heart-rock itself. Both Nyarla and Buryldanji were young, fit and healthy and made good mileage on the first day. On the first night alone together, after eating, Buryldanji expressed a concern that he had withheld in respect to the Fethafoot elders he'd met with. As they sat, quietly enjoying the various and many night sounds and starry night above, the young man finally found his gumption and raised his concern.

"Did the Fethafoot elders not understand what I told them?" he said to her in all seriousness. "Sending a young woman, even as capable as you seem," he continued warily, "to solve a problem that older men, initiated warriors and medicine men failed at," he said, looking quizzically at her as he continued. "Even these, had not been able to do anything about this ... this evil terror! My own elders may not believe that your clan would send only one – and a young woman at that, you see – so I kind of wondered why they would send ... you?" he said lamely ...

The usual test

Nyarla, unsurprised by such doubt, just smiled, rolled her eyes a little in his direction and asked, "Could *you* lose me here at night do you think? Oh Great Warrior!" she said cheekily, which was bold for *any* woman, especially for one so obviously young. Buryldanji laughed out loud then covered his mouth in embarrassment. He was the finest hunter and tracker of his clan. He'd won several events involving tests just like this young woman's challenge, in both his tribe and clan competitions and against very experienced warriors from several lands around his own. Thus, with the perfected humility that winners often possess, he said, "I do not skite Nyarla, but no-one could find me in any part of our land, if I did not wish to be found." He looked at her confidently, with a small smile and flash of sparkling white teeth in his jet-black face.

It was decided between them that Buryldanji would go off in any direction, with a one-moon-shadow start [Fethafoot working night is divided into 10 moon-shadow units, against any tree's shadow movement across the ground] and then, they would see if Nyarla could find him. Buryldanji smiled confidently to himself and set out into the darkness. He used his excellent hunting concealment skills to move around the campfire behind Nyarla and at first, he headed directly back in the direction they had come. Next he used his own fresh footprints walking forward to walk backwards on, until he was near some rocky ground where he jumped almost three metres sideways and grabbed a tree branch to swing up and through the branches. He climbed through the tree until he was over a hard-packed wallaby track that he had spied earlier. He carefully and quietly pulled some small branches with their leaves from the tree, platted them together and quickly laced them with nimble fingers that *saw* in the dark as well as his sharp eyes. He had made a leaf-mat, which he threw on the hard-packed game trail below. Then he lowered himself down and landed softly on the mat to disguise any landing sound and deep foot indents.

Buryldanji smiled proudly and confidently to himself. He stepped to a rock, lifted his mat and moved off like a part of the land that he was: quick and silent, sliding over rocks and sharp clumps of grasses, until he was at the small ridgeline that he had spotted before he left the campfire. He moved along the slight rocky ridge on the darkest side, lithely and low to the ground so that his silhouette couldn't be seen. He was now a good distance away from Nyarla and the campfire. He searched around and found a small cave-like indent in the rock and settled his back into that, to watch back to where the firelight showed the distance he'd come – and an empty camp.

Young Buryldanji had to clamp his hands over his mouth, as it was all he could do not to laugh aloud at this young girl searching for him. But he was to wait for an hour, with no young girl searching that he could see or hear, his own body becoming stiff and cold from the lack of movement. Although he'd never admit it, Buryldanji was becoming a bit nervous himself. He didn't really like being in the dark, outside and alone and, an irritating insect kept bothering him while he was trying his best to stay as still as possible and not give Nyarla any tiny hint as to his whereabouts. The annoying insect would not leave him alone however. It kept landing on his back and neck and bothering him so much that he finally had to move slightly to brush it off.

As he did so, he choked back a very un-warrior-like scream, when he felt a small hand touching him where he'd thought the insect was on his neck. He turned slowly with his heart thudding in his ribs and there she was; right behind him, smiling that gentle smile and in her hand, a twig that she had been tormenting him with for more than a few minutes.

What he had thought was an insect had been her all the time. Now appropriately and deeply humbled, he walked with her back to the camp and although he desperately wanted to know how she had found him so easily and then got so close without him knowing, his pride would not let him ask just yet.

Buryldanji slept well that night and did not hear Nyarla flit back through the bush and circle the camp to check for anything that could be a problem for them on this important journey. Nyarla rested also during the night, although in a trance-like state that gave good rest to her body, but allowed her spirit to unite with her family elders and together discern any disturbances in the Dreaming lines in front of her ...

Across several Dreaming lands

As they walked and talked the following day, curiosity finally got the better of Buryldanji's pride and he asked her how she had done that so easily, when he had won contests at evasion concealment and detection, against the best hunters and trackers in quite a large area. For the first time since they'd left, Nyarla laughed openly and her laugh was a ringing thing of beauty in itself; a free and joyous sound, at amity with the familiar beauty around them in the land. She stopped and turned, although the spark never left her eyes as she told him seriously: "Never ever gamble with a 'family' member." Nyarla looked him straight in the eye. "I straight out cheated and followed you from the moment you left and turned away from the fire," she smiled, and continued more seriously. "Our work requires stealth, cunning and using every advantage possible, to achieve the fastest and best possible outcome from any set of circumstances."

As they began moving along again, Nyarla explained more. "The clan work we do is often fraught with danger and regularly violent," she said. "It's a world where fast, pure action speaks louder than words, more often than not. Although," she paused, "shameless people often find that being violent against the family often meant that they would not, or could not, ever do so again ... ever!" She turned and moved off again.

Buryldanji thought on her explanation as they walked on through that day, although it didn't explain how she could get so close to him without him hearing or smelling anything, despite his trusted senses that had always worked so well for him in the past, which had been wide open; breathlessly alert, for any slight disturbance to the night. But Nyarla gave only that explanation and then kept up an incredible speed that wearied even a young and fit Buryldanji, after several days and long nights of it.

Both were keen of ear and eye and thus, food supplies seemed to come to them rather than they having to hunt for it at all. The game and 'bush-tucker' never seemed to actually abate as they moved further into Queensland, toward the Northern Territory; rather, it just changed species, according to the land and what it gave the animals to survive. They ate meat once a day, usually near evening, and only stopped to kill, prepare, cook and rest for a short time, although Buryldanji noticed that Nyarla kept constant watch on the surroundings, even when resting. During the day, they gathered as they walked, observing the well-known signs of edible roots, berries, nuts, grubs and many small lizards as they went. The smaller lizard kills were hung in their hair until the main meal, when they would go onto the coals and become tasty fried lizard 'nuggets' …

Shopping along the way

While this food-gathering activity can be told in a brief paragraph, it is worth pausing and zooming in for a moment, if only to give some idea of the perfect knowledge and grace of this pair as they walked the land. The pace they maintained was as fast as an Olympic walking athlete without the exaggerated "I'm not *really* running" gait. The ongoing perusal of the whole environment as they moved through it, was merely a flick of the eye or head toward any small movement, or atypical colour, shape or movement in their immediate vicinity. The actual, swift lithe movements used to seize a lizard or other small fast-food on the move was pure poetry in motion: a turned eye, a step or swing of body to one side or the other while moving; the bend to grasp, kill and place in the hair, all one swift movement without pause in forward momentum. Perhaps this food gathering is more easily explained via the analogy of Adam and Eve in The Garden, as in the old Jewish Bible stories of these innocents, taking sustenance as needed.

To an outside observer, the casual attainment of this marvellous takeaway food source and their knowledge of the bush tucker around them would have been breathtaking in its range. That history of 50,000 years of experienced practical knowledge allowed them to make quick progress across the land without stopping to hunt for provisions. Crossing so many tribal lands usually meant days of talk and sometimes etiquette required, even a night of dance. However, Nyarla surprised Buryldanji again and stopped for nothing. Most tribes they passed didn't know of their passing unless Nyarla wanted something – some small piece of information, or once, a particular coloured clay, or other things that she wouldn't discuss with him. She often had silent meetings with bony old wise men in the dead of night, where Nyarla seemed to be treated as an equal. It was very confusing to him, as in his own clan;

women had no say in any of the important decisions. Wisely, the young warrior didn't ask his companion about that discrepancy – Buryldanji was still hurting from the casual defeat in the challenge he had set …

A rest stop

As they neared their destination – in a time that would have shocked to death latter-day explorers Burke and Wills – both young warriors were still in prime condition; this in itself was a sorry exposé on the ignorance and arrogance of the later colonial explorers who refused the food-gifts the aboriginal people that lived in the area offered. Burke and Wills probably would have survived, except that apparently Burke felt that it was beneath him to deal with the "Blacks", or so the story goes.

Meanwhile, Buryldanji stood amazed at the effortless endurance of this young woman he accompanied. She was short, although his estimation of her skills and prowess in observation, hunting and gathering, while moving day and night, totally outgrew her physical stature by his reckoning and he genuinely enjoyed listening and learning from her as they moved across the land. On an evening a few days later, as the burning orange sun sank below the semi-desert landscape and the sweet coolness of the inland night began to permeate their senses, they stopped and made what was for Nyarla, a bona fide camp. She had chosen the site as usual, although this site seemed to be chosen for restful pleasure, something that had not taken place since they began the journey.

They were near a waterhole in what is nowadays the Simpson Desert, on Wankangurru land. Flowering trees and plentiful foods surrounded them, starting with a lone, fully burdened black-apple tree. There were large big-claw, native freshwater crayfish in the muddy water, and tasty sand goanna tracks coming in for water. There were shield-shrimp, whose hardy eggs could roll around in the dry desert dust for up to 10 years, waiting for water to spur them to fast-growing life in their thousands. There were the Bulyum grubs that gave away their secret positions in tree trunks, with the sawdust they left at the base of the tree as they bored in to begin their hungry metamorphosis into a moth; and very tasty on the coals or partaken raw. There was even a nest of the small stingless indigenous bees in a tree, within reach of the ground. Standing on his tiptoes, Buryldanji could see the little sacs of honey, which were valued so much for medicine, healing wounds and its sweet taste, just inside the dark hollow of the nest.

For both Nyarla and Buryldanji, it was like being in a modern-day motel with food and drink virtually on tap. Quickly and efficiently, they hunted and gathered together, cleaned the food and themselves, then made a cooking fire on top of a small indent in the ground, which would become their earth oven. In that clever, practical device, they steamed a snake and a goanna and sat Bulyum, seed and some nuts on the coals at the side of the fire. Soon the tantalising scents puffing out from their earth oven told them that the meat was done and ready. They sat cross-legged either side of the small smokeless fire that Nyarla had taught Buryldanji to make. They ate until they were full and satisfied. It took a few minutes to clean themselves and then their camp, a necessary chore because of the various semi-desert dwelling animals that would forage for any easy leftovers and the many biting insects that would forage on them, if they didn't wash off the food scents. They were done with the repast duties before the moon began to rise …

A man and a woman alone on the land

Buryldanji was so relaxed after the sumptuous meal that he almost forgot why they were travelling together. One look at Nyarla's thoughtful face though, brought back the gravity of the trip and the knowledge of the care that Nyarla would take, now that they were in a few days' walk of the recent events that brought Nyarla and her family to his lands. As they sat and pondered the future and what it might hold, Nyarla surprised Buryldanji by telling him they would be parting ways the next day. "I will have to go on alone from here," she said, eyes looking at something, or somewhere that he could not fathom. He looked carefully at the lithe young woman sitting cross-legged across the fire from him. She was very beautiful to his minds-eye and the mantle of maturity that she carried with her, only served to raise his young man's need and want, to possess her immediately. He would never allow that to show however; this young woman was a Fethafoot no matter what else he saw in her.

Nyarla tilted her head to one side and looked across at him with those strange and lovely young-old eyes, from under a thick hanging lock of her shiny black hair that fell across her face and hid one eye. "It's best for you and your family to not be seen with me at all, now that we are close," she explained, again moving her head and allowing her hair to fall so beautifully, almost seductively over her eyes and breasts. "If the shameful one is as powerful and knowledgeable about local activities as everyone seems to think, then it's wise that the usual traveling storytellers carry no news about a stranger turning up in the area, with a local; especially a lone young woman," she said. Meanwhile, poor Buryldanji, his black skin blushing deeply, tried desperately to keep his small lap-cover down where it should be, but her voice was so sultry and her face and body looked so soft and inviting in the lick of light from the fire's small flames that he had to shift uncomfortably to cover his rising manhood.

Unable to miss the change in his posture, Nyarla flicked the slightest glance down to that area and continued on, as if his rising manhood were completely natural. "My family give no warning to an adversary and we know that surprise is one of the deadliest weapons when fighting any powerful foe," she told him. Buryldanji, however, didn't seem to be listening. And although he'd had secret designs and a tiny hope for any type of dalliance with her, Nyarla had given no sign of either attraction, or dislike of him until tonight. She had always behaved with the utmost decorum, as befitted an unbetrothed young woman from another clan. All her actions and words had exampled that the mission was paramount and all else superficial. This night, however, he had noticed her disappearance for a short time and on her return, he could not help but notice that she had bathed her body and combed her hair.

And from the pleasant fresh scent he'd smelled on her upon her return, she must have found some sweet smelling leaf or flower that she rubbed into her hair and over her body, and now Buryldanji, for probably the first time in his adult life, felt strangely nervous. He was unsure whether to make a move or to wait and that hesitation disturbed him greatly, as he was known as a confident lover, as well as for his other skills in his tribe and locally. Nyarla, however, was so vastly different from any other woman he'd ever met, and he realised also that he had been treating her as an equal since they'd left, and this equality she had accepted as completely normal.

Thus, as the moon rose and the Australian semi-desert landscape softened, with the moonlight spreading its luminous silver glow throughout their temporary home, and as the various night animals began their calls, Nyarla again surprised him. She lay down on the bed of scented, green leafy bushes she'd gathered and boldly asked him to lay with her, which the eager young man did with almost indecent haste. She slowed his eager passion and offered him smoke from a bone pipe, filled with what he thought may be dried, ground Pitcherii, a naturally growing plant that only grew in certain areas of Australia and that was prized by clever-men and elders for its other-worldly effect ...

Seduced and lovin it

As often happens when a young man and a young woman are together alone at night in a comfortable space in the open air, they talked and touched; and she teased him mercilessly as only a woman who knew her own power could do. Buryldanji was sure he was near to death. He was uncertain as to whether he was excited, nervous or actually dying, as his poor heart was beating so rapidly and with so much force that he felt a little faint. All he could hear at this moment was his roaring heartbeat and his own panting breath. And, coming from what seemed like all around him, her soft and silvery entreaties that spoke directly to his male essence and his manhood – soft, ululating yearnings for him to touch and kiss and envelop her own lascivious desires.

Still dazed and confused and not wanting to sully her radiance with his unwashed body, Buryldanji began to stand. "I am unwashed and ..." Nyarla stopped him, taking hold of his arm. "I've cleansed myself for you my heart, this night," she cooed, "and I want you with your male-ness and power intact," she said, in a much coarser growl as she pulled him back down close to her rapidly warming body. "Mmm! I love your wild smell and your stiff, crinkly hair and I like your easily fathomed, honest passion for me," she said, holding him tightly to her slowly writhing body. Buryldanji was rock hard – all over. All doubt was gone. His manhood stood attentively, quivering between their bodies, while he began to kiss and touch her – *truth be known*, he thought – *as he had been dreaming about, since their journey had begun* ...

Not alone

Their lovemaking was like no other Buryldanji had ever known. She seemed to bewitch him with her urgent cries that began to sound as though several wild animals were with them: a dingo panting after running down its prey, kangaroo rutting, birds calling to mates to couple. As they fell into the dance of life together, the sounds around them strengthened, becoming more piercing. Although caught up in the wild passion, Buryldanji let his eyes drift away from her and the soft beauty of her body underneath him for a moment, and he gasped as he looked out to the surrounding area. Around the light of their small fire were animals of every type and description. They were watching the pair intently: bobbing, dancing, crying and grunting, as though they too were taking part in something much bigger than a mere coupling.

The idea that nature itself was involved in this coupling; that the girl-woman Nyarla was in fact much more than she seemed to be, excited him as never before and he drove his manhood's length and his whole body into her overwhelming female desire. Time and everything around him disappeared, except the sensual touch of live flesh given freely and the arousing smells and sounds of their coupling. Nyarla did things to his stiff manhood that should have been impossible. She rippled and washed over him as though the hard Mother Earth they lay upon was softly loving caressing and embracing him. The scents from her body drowned him in a wild orgy of frenetic dance that drove his spirit and mind back; back to his Dreaming place. Even as he felt the hot softness of the woman's skin and sensual body underneath him, Buryldanji *saw* his clan's totem animals and sacred places in his mind with such clarity that he might have been there, in the Dreaming with them.

Then Nyarla suddenly grunted: arms and legs, thighs, lips and hands crushing him into her while she lifted his whole body off the ground, as she called out a guttural earthen embrace of life and death – in language that he was certain had not been heard for many, many years, maybe generations – as he too released his exploding passion. Buryldanji fulfilled his own involuntary, shuddering, little death with an ease and power that his over-sensitive body already longed to duplicate, though his heart and mind knew already that he would never feel the same depth of physical delight and sensual acuity again without her. Then, curled against her warmth, he slept deeply and peacefully …

Waking up alone

When he awoke, although it was early and the sun had not yet risen, she was gone. He had heard and felt nothing, although they had slept together after the invigorating experience, which still played on through his mind and tingled through his fingers, thighs and sore little spear. He looked for her track, but found only the animals that he was not sure had been there at all last night. He now knew that they had been real at least, but of his young female Fethafoot travelling companion there was no sign.

Nyarla had set off just a few hours after she had lain with Buryldanji. She knew that she must go quickly and that Buryldanji must go back to his clan and let the elders that had sent him know that there was a Fethafoot attending to their request. The only thing that she had asked of him was to not to let anyone know that the warrior was female.

In her last recent talk with one of the old Clever-men, she'd found out the lay of the land in front of her and many of the secret places that could help her with the problem of the shameful one. Nyarla now felt quietly confident that her path would take her to a spot where she could keep lookout for anyone or anything travelling around that part of the country. In one instance, the vital knowledge gained on the trip was as precise as to a particular Eagle family that lived in the area that warned of any movement in that area, if one knew what to look for. She knew that she had to be stealthily quiet and use all her skill to leave no track.

She would eat without fire and would drink at night at several secret waterholes, which had been revealed in stories to her. These stories told of landmarks and directions to tiny underground waterholes that were often not in the knowledge bank of the local people anymore. Some of these places had not been mentioned for generations and she was sure that the bad spirit, if that was what this shameful thing was, had no idea that she could live comfortably in the area while she tracked it and decided what she would do to stop its grisly reign of terror …

CHAPTER 3

12 KILOMETRES AWAY – CENTRAL AUSTRALIA, BURYLDANJI, THE RUNNER'S CLAN CAMP

Buryldanji had been home for a day now and was soon to be interviewed by the elders who had sent him for Fethafoot help. As desert day fell into night and the hunters and women and children gatherers came slowly back to camp in ones and twos, carrying all manner of food, Buryldanji's heart leapt in his breast at the warm and familiar talk and murmured conversations of his beloved clan...

The land

For his generation, the land was not as dry as it is now and on return from hunting and gathering there was always much merriment and good-natured ribbing. Especially of any hunter who had done some brave or stupid thing; or over any small event that had caused the women and children to break out into their routine bellyaching laughter during the day. One particular event that Buryldanji heard and that had almost everyone in fits was the story about the hunter who had followed the women and children to scare them and had walked straight into a hornet's nest while trying to creep up on them. Instead of scaring the women and children as he rose up fast from his hiding position, he knocked a hornet nest with his head and was last seen by the group, dashing off into the desert in the direction of a waterhole, swinging his arms and hands wildly about his head while hornets attacked him viciously. He was still swollen about his eyes and neck now, and every time the children saw him, they shouted out his name as 'the great hornet nest hunter' to the amusement of everyone, except the man himself.

At the appointed time, Buryldanji went to the elder's fire and sat to wait and be asked about his trip and their request. In usual Aboriginal custom, he was not asked immediately about the main outcome, but had to tell of whom he had met and the details of the land he had travelled: what tribes he had met and whom they were related to. He was asked about waterholes, rivers, creeks and hunting issues.

Finally, as they had dealt with his news – needed for any other travelling through that area – he was asked about the Fethafoot meeting. However, he was held back again as one elder asked first, about who was there and who had passed; who was leading various clans and who had married, prior to the main topic. Buryldanji knew this was not procrastination on the elders' part, but a way of gaining true information that would be integrated into news for that part of the country, which in itself was very important to the overall and up-to-date knowledge for travellers and extended family. Thus, he sat still, answering clearly with patience and respect while all this went on, despite his eagerness to tell about the warrior and the skills and power exampled while travelling together.

When finally, someone casually asked him what the Fethafoot would do, he quickly told of the coming of the warrior and of her immense knowledge, power and cunning, although he omitted gender altogether, as Nyarla had requested. The elders were a little surprised to hear that the clan had sent only one person and such a young one at that, although Buryldanji's quiet confidence gave them some assurance as to a possible ending to the bad spirit's days of terror. They told him that another woman had gone missing since the young warrior Gilgardi and that only a few of the missing people's bodies had ever been found. They also explained that the whole area was now more scared than ever and all local groups were waiting in trepidation for the next disappearance or skulduggery by this evil spirit: "all except" one elder said, "for some of the naive, angry young men who had already seriously wounded one of their own, in their brave attempts to find and kill the terror scaring everyone," he explained.

After Buryldanji's meeting, the elders thanked him for his patience and valuable information and asked him politely to leave them, while they discussed what was surely to come. Every elder there knew of the Fethafoot clan and its workings and they were very happy to have the powerful clan handling a problem that had perplexed them for many moons now. As usual, the elders themselves completed the meeting with a dance that thanked the Great Spirit for bringing their son home safely. The dance and accompanying song also requested the Great Spirit's own wisdom and strength, to bolster the heart of the brave warrior that would have to find and go up against the evil thing in their midst...

Eerwa

At that moment the unconscionable thing, Eerwa; The Terror – as it thought so proudly of itself – was just a few kilometres away, forcing down a pungent concoction of gelatinous blood and warm urine from its latest victim. Eerwa was very satisfied with himself and confident that the power he had gained from his last dark ceremony and the great cloud of fear that he had created roundabout, was strong enough now to keep all the local medicine men's spiritual searching totally blinded. Eerwa had no idea that the Fethafoot were looking for him and if he had known, he would not have cared, believing himself to be more powerful than any other powerful sorcerers in the land now: hadn't he killed and eaten the souls of some of the best and strongest hunters and warriors in the local dreaming lands!

So close to fulfilling its dark dream now, his dark spirit became utterly devoted to finishing his malevolent undertaking and thus, gain all the power that he could ever want or need. It was a burning desire that had overtaken everything else, ever since he'd fulfilled the obligation that had started him on this dark path: a routine fight over a woman from a clan near here that had ended in anger, bloodshed and death. His own obligation for that death was to have killed and disappeared his first victim.

But in carrying out that first killing, Eerwa discovered that he loved killing: slowly and secretly – and the brilliant, screaming light of his victim's helpless fear gave him the deepest, most profound gratification of any physical ecstasy that he'd ever known. From that fateful point onward, *he* became *it* and as it moved from eating The Mother's bounty to raw human flesh and drinking human blood, swift mental deterioration followed. The man he was no longer lived and that which had taken over, had gone rapidly insane and now believed that it had such power that it could take what it wanted and never again be obligated to anyone at all. The angry ignorant man, who had requested the initial slaying, didn't know or suspect that the obligation he'd asked of his strange uncle had now distorted into the frightening apparition that stalked the land, and was feared throughout.

Eerwa had one last task he needed to perform and then he believed, he would finally rule his world – with no one and nothing able to stand before him. That last task however, left him slightly nervous. He had to travel across open ground, to a secret place of old and terrible memories. It was a place where many warriors had died together, from what most believed were supernatural forces, in a terrifying event that had occurred several generations before. Eerwa believed that his skill at concealment and his ill-begotten magical ability to move over the land undetected would allow him to make it to the location and then, fulfil the last ritual and finalise his Dreaming-seditious undertaking.

Thus, he rested in his vile underground lair and gathered his power about him for two full days before he moved again. Though in his haste and hunger for more and more raw power, he was ignorant of the fact that his claimed cave was still part of The Mother and had, since he'd moved in with his grisly possessions, also become a space that wept silent Dreaming tears for his victims; those trapped and held from their proper burial rites. Thus, unknowingly, Eerwa had caught the attention of a second powerful entity – a primordial, relentless enemy – much more powerful than his own power-blinded, lust-gripped eyes could ever fathom …

A soft foot on hard rock

A short distance away on Uluru itself, and right above what is now termed *The Brain*: a weathered, physical image of the Great Spirit's coming-of-age protector in the physical world, Nyarla sat directly above the men's sacred place, where her keen eyes watched and waited for any unusual movement or activity around her. From here, she could see for two, nearly three days walk all around the Heart-rock. From here in normal times, Nyarla knew she would see old men and boys go in and out from the sacred caves below. She would have heard the cries of exultation while young men received their tribal and skin markings on their chests and shoulders. She would have seen eager young boys enter, keen to take their place on the path to becoming initiated men, and listened to their youthful cries of pain as they passed through initiation. Now though, because of the shameless one who had literally stopped all rites and custom in the area, the whole area around the monolith was deathly quiet. There were neither sounds nor smoke coming from even the women's sacred places here, and those places were usually very noisy with many comings and goings from daylight to dusk.

After two long days of watching and waiting and spotting nothing out of the ordinary, Nyarla saw a dark spot in the distant sky that she deciphered as an Eagle. As it got closer, she saw that the bird matched the colouring, size and territory that one of the wise men she'd met on the journey had told her to watch out for. Even far away on the desert sands, the bird's actions told her clearly that something was moving below her – and trying to move furtively; betrayed by the fashion in which the eagle flew and by its shrill, piercing, annoyed call that drifted across the Desert with the wind. Nyarla knew that this would usually mean a secret initiation trial, a secret liaison between a man and woman, perhaps even from a *wrong* skin group; but with fear holding most movement and all ceremony at bay around Heart-rock, it may also mean that the mysterious, malicious predator was moving out from its lair at last.

One thing was certain: the eagle was not hunting, but watching something move over its terrain – and it was not happy about it scaring the rodents and small animals back undercover, where it couldn't get at them. Nyarla's eyes, ears and intuition also told her that this bird was a mother and very unhappy at the intrusion, as she needed to find food for her young.

The Fethafoot decided not to start out from her hide just yet, in case whatever it was, was completely harmless and the thing she was waiting for slipped away, while she chased an eager invention of her mind. She was quite comfortable in her present surroundings, with plenty of water and food as it had rained recently and there were pools and trickling waterfalls all over the Heart-rock. There were also tasty shield-shrimp that could be eaten whole uncooked and still many small lizards and even small frogs that could be eaten raw when need arose. Nyarla also knew that although she could not see the thing moving on the ground that far away, it might be able to see her silhouette against the sky, because of her height above the flat open ground below. She was fairly certain that the thing or spirit would be watching every movement possible, as it had already eluded the best hunter-trackers in this area – and for a long time.

The cave-like structure that Nyarla waited in was cool and she had a back path out if she needed – that didn't allow her form to be seen from anywhere on the ground below. Nyarla thought briefly about the horrific violence that the thing had carried out. There never was good reason for mortal violence, however, as with her predecessors, she felt that if it came to any type of confrontation – as was now certain to occur, the whys and wherefores would not enter into her actions to guard and protect her beloved people and sacred land. The clan believed that violence against their society was often best rewarded with stronger, even fatal violence, dependent on the severity and that the lessons learned by surviving peoples, were often worth more than the life of any individual, shameless one...

The Clan's tenets

Such was the belief system of the Fethafoot, and its practical reasoning and actions had shaped many of Heart-rock's clans and tribe's ethics and morals out of pure fear, much as the English Bible would put fear into the hearts of the shameless under its laws later on. The word "shameless" was used considerably, to speak of people who exampled morals and ethics to the detriment, rather than the good of *the* people. If you were known as shameless, it was like being called a person with no personal or tribal dignity – characteristics that were held in awe by her people since time began. Without individual dignity, the elders said, there was no group future and there could be no genuine contentment in the people. Dignity in a person provided a space – they said – for a lasting

23

individual fulfilment that smoothed the path of accomplishment for the entire tribe …

An ignorant Clan client

Lost in mind, spirit and his search for personal power, Eerwa had no such dignity. He had allowed his thirst for the darkest aspects of power to overwhelm his humanity and, as Nyarla sat and pondered his probable brief future, he himself grinned arrogantly, totally unaware of the judgment being pronounced on his deeds as he crossed the barren land on his way to the place of death, where no-one else would set foot for at least another two generations. The elders at the time had decreed that it would take five generations for Earthmother to cleanse the site. No human, nor clever-man's power they felt, could cleanse such terrible calamity and in fact, only the performance of *her* natural cleansing it was said, could ever make that place habitable for humans to ever cross again.

Eerwa was almost to his place of power. He could feel the vibrant force of the many swift, brutal, ugly and confused deaths, long before he reached the outskirts of the stone circle where the event had transpired. He'd noticed the eagle that he'd disturbed earlier, seemingly calling to him from high in the air, *to warn him away from this evil place*, he'd thought, although deluded by his dark misshapen power, the Terror laughed arrogantly at its shrill warning calls …

Nyarla's not laughing

Still watching keenly with eyes that were virtually as effective as the eagle's celebrated sight, Nyarla saw the predator swoop and followed its graceful form as it veered away from an area, which from where she stood, looked like a small round darker spot in the burnt orange sand. This latest sign from the mother eagle was the best indication of any stealthy movement that she'd seen since beginning her watch and the slight warrior moved out of her hide and quickly slid, hands and feet slowing her quick descent down the rough sandstone of Heart-rock, to the hot sandy terrain below.

Once down, she knelt on the ground in a small area of boulders that protected from any view and after taking various items from the small hide-pouch she wore, Nyarla began her purification ceremony. She knew that the eagle had spotted something that she didn't like or understand, revealed by its erratic movements and its soft but discordant alarm call. It was a tell-tale call that the warrior picked up infrequently, as it drifted toward Heart-rock on the wind currents that the graceful creature used so elegantly to move quickly across its desert territory.

Now that she was purified for the coming encounter, Nyarla had one last act to perform before she went after the thing that had alarmed the eagle. She sat cross-legged, gathered her spiritual strength and with an act of will, fused her spirit mind and body together as one, calling on the boundless energy that flowed from the Mother to power her need. Using her Clan trained skill, the young warrior used her subtle power of animal mind bonding for a meeting of minds and thus, the warrior's spirit spoke to the eagle's spirit ...

It's a Fethafoot thing

A kilometre up and away from Heart-rock, the great bird suddenly dropped several metres toward the earth as it felt her light delicate presence materialise within her. Then, understanding the Fethafoot's need, the big bird flew directly toward the ignorant two-leg who dared defy the angry ancient spirits at that place: where she had restricted even her young from visiting. From this high airborne view, Nyarla saw that the skulking wanderer a short distance away was indeed the shameless one she pursued. Seeing him through the eagle's eyes, she recognised the dark foreboding aura, which the eagle saw, was clearly unlike any normal creature: its dark swirling inner spirit moved and struggled around the being. It was as if the imprisoned human spirit was desperately trying to escape from the insanity that the shameless one had born and bred within itself.

Understanding that its work was complete now, the eagle banked smoothly to catch a thermal updraught and within minutes, Nyarla was back within her body and moving rapidly and silently across the sands toward her unsuspecting client: in the flesh ...

The circle of stones

Eerwa had finally reached his destination, seemingly without discovery and had begun the initial rites that would culminate in a crucial night ceremony, to gather the power and souls of the long dead to his own use. Now that he was physically here, even the long dead seemed to shy away from him and he laughed out an ugly depraved barking sound to feel such fear from these powerful land-locked spirits. He and they knew that once he completed his ceremony, they would be in *his* power forever; while-ever he walked and breathed.

What Eerwa the Terror didn't know, was that a terrible retribution awaited him when he finally did pass over, as these old souls trapped on earth would not take lightly to being used by the ignorant shameless. He was also unaware that at that very moment, a Fethafoot was squatting behind a small bush almost within spitting distance of him; naked, but for a petite hairless animal skin that covered the dark triangle of her pubic hair and her small warrior's bag that hung between her sweat moistened breasts.

Nyarla squat silently and prepared herself, slowing her breathing, blending her body within the four elements and drawing more and more of The Mother's vast power to her self as she prepared to face the thing that called itself Eerwa …

While the world turns

That being had completed the parts of the rite that he could do in the daylight and after setting a small smokeless fire to be lit later in the sinister ceremony, he carefully wiped any trace of his activity and movement from around the area and walked carefully toward a shade tree, just a short distance away from the stone circle. He too now sat and waited for the coming night and the completion of his foul rite.

Though satisfied with his preparations, Eerwa still felt wary, exposed, almost entangled in the vast openness of the desert and the wide open sky and away from his stinking death scented lair and his beloved lifeless and decaying conquests. He barely moved as the sun sank and the evening began to cool, accustomed to preying on human prey that watched constantly for any movement as a natural survival instinct. He knew his concealment skills, strong arm and good eye could keep him safe from any locals stupid enough to seek or pursue him. He also had his killing spears and a heavy woomera with him and although he felt fairly safe now that his favourite part of day was arriving, he kept a wary eye on any slight movement around.

But soon Eerwa – The Terror, began to relax; there was nothing to stop his gathering of power from these powerful spirits now. He was so close to becoming a force of nature that he could feel it in his bones …

A palpable force at a natural event

Nearby, another very resilient force of nature sat unmoving and patient, watching him. And she knew something else that he didn't – aside from the fact that she had found him – and, she was going to use it to full advantage as soon as the eerie natural event began. A once in three-generation event, known to the Clan as Djkapa-boorunduh, would occur this night. What we know as the Aurora Australis, or the Southern Lights would reflect in the desert sky from what was known as 'the great White in the south' on *this* night, and Nyarla was confident that Eerwa had no idea that he had chosen to fulfil his ghastly mission at the same time as this infrequent event. Nyarla had read the Mother's signs and now knew

26

that this very night, the night sky would light up in an awesome display that would frighten all, and keep most close to home and campfire. Ignorant Eewar she noted had already placed his obsessions facing toward the north and away from the south, where the lights would soon make a startling and dazzling spectacle in the sky. Nyarla also reasoned that she had to act prior to Eerwa taking the grand event as a sign of his own power, and a dark blessing on his nefarious activities. Thus, *she* would gain the advantage of its surprise occurrence …

Opposing forces meet

As the sun set and the time approached for Eerwa to begin, he searched carefully around him before moving slowly back toward the circle of stones that marked the old death place. Confident now, he began arranging his stolen human body parts – dried and semi-dried out now and looking more malevolent than ever, as they were only almost-identifiable caricatures of human parts; flesh that was once a part of living, breathing people. Eerwa began to lay his grisly objects on the ground, placing each in the correct positions for his sacrilegious ceremony. He laid out the now vile items – some covered in dried faeces, others with dried and blood-soaked pubic hair wrapped around them – several soaked in his victim's urine – then he lit his small fire, stood, stretched his big, hairy body to its extremities – and then, Eerwa began his dance to capture the dread power here.

He moved always to the left, against custom, to create what was in his mind, a vortex of anti-energy to conquer and thus allow him to steal the power of the dead from the old restricted circle. As he danced, lost in his dark vile fantasies of unlimited power, his nemesis rose too and began to dance – and to move in exactly identical patterns. Her feet arms hands, her whole body matched Eerwa's measured step as her slim sinuous body moved, congruent with the desert night and her oblivious adversary. Anyone watching this macabre dance, with its gruesome centrepiece of rotting body parts lit by flickering firelight, would have thought that Nyarla led the steps. Her intuition to follow and yet to be in motion before him was uncanny.

Her predictive moves to a ceremonial dance that Eerwa himself had developed – as he moved first one way, then another; up, down and around with heavy feet thumping the earth to his own frenetic pulsations – were simply spellbinding. While Eerwa knew the steps he had created, Nyarla, moving minutely beforehand – if that deed were possible – seemed to inhabit the dance's steps. Her small taut dark breasts shone from a film of sweat that ran down onto the darker nipples, which rose in response to the moisture and cool night air and then on again, down her flat shining belly and into her dark, sweat-filmed pubic area. She moved in such svelte corresponding steps to Eerwa that the Terror could still only hear his own slide, slap and thump as his feet followed the ritual moves he'd created for this ceremony ...

Lights in the sky

Nyarla had also been keeping one eye on the sky for any sign of the dazzling display and now, she observed a tiny flickering light that had begun to play on the horizon at ground level to the south. She wait until Eerwa turned and in perfect time with his movements, she danced right up to behind him, still following his every move perfectly – sliding from her cover to behind his back so smoothly, it seemed as if a common night shadow had detached itself from the land and moved to a better position.

And as he turned from the fire, she turned also, staying behind and with him: his silent, constant shadow partner. Then, as they swirled together around the small ceremonial fire, the slight mirroring shadow's slender hand moved slightly, perversely out of time – to cast a small cloud of crushed Pituri leaves, mixed with a rare crushed root from her pouch, directly into the flames.

As Eerwa turned once more to complete his ceremonial dance, Nyarla floated unseen back to the darkness outside his flickering firelight. This incredible doppelganger feat had taken no more than a few seconds and to give credit where it's due – to the Fethafoot training that any master martial artist would have been in awe of – Nyarla had executed this veiled performance, while keeping exact pace and time with Eerwa's intricate movements; and somehow staying outside of his sense and field of view.

Thus, in his ecstasy of prospective ceremonial success, Eerwa the Terror had no inkling that anyone had, or could ever have been close enough to alter his very senses. And now, via the smoke rising slowly from the fire, the self-proclaimed Death Adder and The Terror would find such altered state of mind as the combined drugs gave: irrepressible. As he moved around his trophies, through and across the smoke-trail carrying the drug, it began to weave its way into his bloodstream. There was no distinctive smell, no warning to his senses that anything was different; had changed at all. His breathing was heavy from the exertion of the dance, pulling the drug deep into his lungs. His heart rate began to speed up. His pupils dilated and the drug's psychedelic effect forced a unique, bizarre perspective on his mind's eye almost instantly. His only grasped perception became a desperate haunting look at the darkness of the night that abruptly took over his awareness – a condition and view that his various victims might have recognised only too well in the ensnared shock and disbelief in their own terrified anguished eyes …

An irrevocable opportunity

As with all Fethafoot judgments, Nyarla understood that she must give her client – now become prey – a chance to repent his actions and to willingly pay for his crimes. At this instant, as Eerwa turned instinctively toward her hiding place – not nearly as confident about his powers as he'd been just a few, short minutes before – Nyarla stepped from behind her cover and into his view. For Eerwa, in his drugged, torpid state – and because Nyarla wished it so, it looked as though a small female dingo had suddenly materialised from thin air, right in front of him. He fell backwards gasping and uttered a small cry of fright and wonder, although genuine astonishment was about to overtake his now intensely confused senses.

Nyarla had timed her physical revelation to perfection. As she began to speak to Eerwa, the sky behind her lit up like a surreal pyrotechnics display. The whole horizon behind her had suddenly changed from the starlit darkness of the normal desert night sky, to a blazing kaleidoscope of light and colour, and although Eerwa had heard of such before, he had never seen it or lived it through the eyes of a strong drug – that he was unaware of taking. His eyes now became huge horrified pools, reflecting Nyarla the dingo in front of him, the various changing colours in the sky and his fear and fright at the rapid shocking unfamiliar direction that this night – his supposed night of fulfilment – had suddenly taken.

The dingo spoke – and Eerwa stifled a scream and shuffled backward on his butt, all pride, arrogance and false-dignity departed him. He heard the voice but could not fathom its intent or meaning, just because he was so utterly terrified. The immense light transformations and flickering power across the skies behind the creature, together with the animal talking to him, had thrown his drugged senses into overload. His normal arrogant and forceful attitude vanished into a vacuum, instantly transforming into a childlike panic that he had not felt since his childhood.

Nyarla spoke again, more slowly this time, though still giving Eerwa little time to come to terms with the bizarre situation that she'd shaped. "I know your wants and needs, shameless one," she began again. "I know about your inhuman actions in taking life to gain personal power," it said to him. Eerwa stared in horror at the back-lit, talking dog that came closer yet, forcing him to scramble further back on his hands and buttocks, while staring fearfully at the moving, rainbow-colored night-sky behind the apparition …

The Dreamtime Lores

"The old people gave us the Law, directly from the ancient creation spirits," it said, continuing to speak, while moving closer with its red furry head tilted sideways and its sharp ears pointed straight at him. "*They* gave us the proper ways of conduct, which the Great Spirit has set out for the people to live by," it said gravely. It spoke the names of the revered ancient laws and finally, asked the *old* questions as she stood directly in front of him, still sitting on the ground, his hands out toward her between them in shock and disbelief.

"Could you change your ways, man of dust? Lose your terrible hunger for power at any cost, man of lust?" the Dingo asked him clearly now. "Can you even see that what you have done is wrong? That it is against every true law of our people," it asked him while its golden predatory eyes gazed deeply into his own sickly, yellow-tinged, wide eyes.

But Eerwa was slowly regaining some of his usual proud arrogance. Crazed thoughts ran wild through his mind. This was just an animal. A Dingo! A four-leg creature to keep him warm on cold nights and kill and eat, if he could find nothing else. He could hardly believe that such an inconsequential animal was judging and questioning him and with the final question, his anger rose in waves, forcing his childish fears down again. He was so full of blind rage that his body began to claim its own movement again and his anger suddenly gushed through him hotly. He groaned and then grunted awfully as he tried to shout out his anger and humiliation and stand; wondering why he was having so much trouble just getting his feet under himself, let-alone speak.

Nyarla moved back as she asked the final questions, giving Eerwa a small space and time to answer any of the questions and to stand and face her, if he could manage that small act at present. To Eerwa, it seemed that the Dingo had moved back to sit staring at him, small doggy head to one side, looking at him and waiting on his answers without blinking – and still, lit up eerily from the cascade of light behind it in the sky.

Then it spoke again. "Would you make reparation to the dead's families, man of dust?" it asked, almost formally, as if it were some respected, elder white-hair sitting in judgment of him …

A base nature

The questions kept coming at him, hitting him physically like war-clubs in a battle against a strong, fearless enemy. "Would you take the punishment that even now may not have to end in your death, man of dust?" it asked. "Could you earnestly state your remorse?" it added. At this final question, with its accompanying possible escape from proper judgment, the spirits of the past warriors in the circle behind them began to moan loudly. Eerwa heard them, although all of his confused senses were focused on Nyarla and her battery of questions. But he could feel their awful power rising behind him and somehow, the sorcerer knew in his heart that they keened and wailed at *any* talk of mercy for him.

Eerwa had almost made it to his knees as Nyarla moved in closer, attended by the strange and powerful light show flickering across the dingo's red fur. Somehow its remorseless fierce presence forced him back further, closer to his fire and once again he found himself on his buttocks on the ground, scrabbling backward and terrified out of his wits. Once more, in the spirit of accepted Clan ritual, Nyarla asked the questions one last time, but instead of any acceptance of wrongdoing or feelings of guilt, Eerwa broke through his shock and abruptly became dangerously, inhumanly angry. His erupting fury broke through his dazed senses, overcoming even the drug's powerful influence momentarily and he leapt to his feet, angry stupefied and frustrated that he could only snarl and spit his defiance at this insignificant ignorant thing attempting to stop *his* dark quest for more power.

Even with the drugs coursing through his body, Eerwa glimpsed his killing spears still lying where he had left them and he moved slyly, staggering closer to them. The enraged sorcerer used his old friend darkness as cover, only moving between the flashing sky's pulsing light show, ignoring the Dingo's droning questions as he gauged the distance to the specific weapon he wanted. Then when he was close enough, he leapt to where they lay with the desperate speed and grace of a cornered animal with nothing left to lose.

From many years of executing this act, the awful *Terror* touched down gracefully and slid the toes of one foot under his favourite spear. He leant lithely back, snapping his leg up, which vaulted the spear through the air to his eager waiting hand, already held back behind his head and shoulders at full stretch. Eerwa knew how lethal he was with this weapon and now he smiled cruelly. All he had to do was point and throw and the pivoting of his shoulder forward, coupled with the force of his pointing arm pushing down would launch the spear with immense force and speed — as if from a Woomera, at this distance. He snarled and launched without hesitation — and with all the force and power he could gather, grunting heavily from the force of his throw. The sound of wind whistling and air pierced by the thrust of his most well balanced killing spear sounded out its deadly vibration in the still night air ...

Talking dog, woman, or spirit?

Eerwa struck like his namesake – the skilfully fast Death-adder serpent – a cruel grin on his terrible black face in anticipation of a slow awful death to the arrogant dingo-thing, who dared to treat *him* like a naughty child. He would leave it to writhe in pain while he finished his ceremony, then when he was full of the dark power he craved so much, he would tear each limb from it, while he asked his own set of hard-edged questions. However, in the few short seconds it took for his deadly missile to reach its target, he saw that the dingo-spirit had simply disappeared. Once again, he'd been beaten easily and again awed shock overtook his furious anger and filled his scarred visage.

There – standing in the dingo's place and just off-line from where his deadly spear had cut through the air – stood a young woman. She didn't speak, she just stood smiling tragically at his attempt to stay alive – without due payment. In her deep golden, ancient eyes however, it was crystal-clear that this woman believed that she knew where this struggle was going and where it would end.

Eerwa became even more furious. That she showed no fear at all and thus, utterly no respect to him – the most feared and powerful magic-man in the whole of this seven-tribe area – struck like a bludgeon at what was left of his already irrational and now drugged mind. That she could creep up on him, transform herself into a dingo and make fun of him – *Eerwa! The Death Adder! The terror of the night: the fearsome devil that had already taken many brave hunters' lives* – utterly shocked him to his core.

To make matters even worse, the arrogant young woman also seemed to already own the powers that he craved so desperately and for which, he had sold and warped his own humanity. This dazed revelation sent him rushing at her like the drugged blood that was pumping feverishly through his veins.

Unfortunately for Eerwa, he was also rushing toward the unpleasant, downward spiral of his own death-song and though he was yet a walking talking, albeit insanely screaming sentient being, two too many ancient powers ranged hard against his recent dark choices ...

An irresistible requiem

Now fully in the spirit herself, Nyarla could feel his death-song looping around them as carelessly casual as this man had chosen to spend his profane life energy. The faint hungry vacuum of his final song swam through the surrounding landscape and trees, waiting for him to catch up: and as he rushed at her, it was there – full of the want of his warm living breath, his blackened male potency and his putrid life-force. Nyarla could feel its hunger, its eagerness for his joining once more to the inevitable cycle of the Dreaming: birth, life, death, judgment, rest and re-birth. And once more, Nyarla felt the old sadness come upon her – the Fethafoot burden of becoming judge and jury and of taking a wasted shameless life to spare more virtuous, deserving lives.

As Nyarla reacted – using her training and power to instantly become a part of the surrounding land and all of The Mother's face that could be seen – Eerwa saw only tiny wavering pieces of the land and trees that he too knew so well, suddenly form up and move toward him like quicksilver. Far, far too quickly, Eerwa felt the almost gentle touch of the finger that she laid softly upon him – as a slight contact on his chest over his heart – and mere moments later; he was on his back staring stupidly at the sky above …

Careful what you wish for

He saw a glorious blue-black desert night sky, filled again with dotted pinpoints of stars in a sky that was quickly regaining its normal balance of central Australian night hues. And as Eerwa lay helpless, he suddenly knew many other things as well, although for the first time in many years, the sorcerer genuinely wished for nothing but blind ignorance. He knew that he was on his back and lying on the earth. He knew that he'd been thoroughly bested by this strangely quiet, powerful young woman and that she had barely touched him, yet he could not move his physically formidable body at all. He also knew he was and should be; very scared of the savage bark of the spirits from the circle he had so casually chosen to desecrate.

They were becoming louder, closer and more real by the second. Powerful old dusty-scented spirits that were now baying for much more than just his flesh and blood. Eerwa could feel their awareness of his burnt, shrivelled soul. Now, too late, he realised that they saw him as an irreligious upstart. A fool who would believe himself to be a power in a land where real power lay everywhere; "though, bound to Law!" the anguished voices howled at him. "Power usually dormant until stirred by nature, or by some ignorant clever-man's meddling and then: uncontrollable," they whispered. Paralysed like his many helpless bound victims, the would-be sorcerer also understood – while listening to the ancient spirit's chatter – that it was this same limitless power, which the Fethafoot had sent against him in the guise of a slender young clever-woman.

The young Fethafoot left him there, bound by power and helpless and although she knew that he was not in as much pain and anguish as his various victims, still she keened in her spirit for his sudden fall toward death at her own hands. She left him paralysed and in fear of his circle-soul being utterly consumed, while the spirits tormented him as he had tormented others. Now that they were on the same spiritual plane, the ancient spirits revealed just how little Eerwa knew of real terror and real power. In his horror and shock, Eerwa also knew now that these ancient spirits had been screaming and groaning to him earlier, because the power he'd already held had been enough to have freed them; enough to enable them to move on. If he had listened and chosen to use his powers for his people rather than against them, then their patient sojourn – locked between life and death – could have been ended …

Be *quiet while you scream*

Every clamouring spirit's voice boomed and screeched at him, tearing into his essence like worms eating his live flesh. "The Path! The Path!" they screamed. "The wrong path you chose!" they shrieked as one. "You took the wrong path! You selfish empty husk of dust! You dry and stupid wrinkled withered spirit!" they cried and writhed in and through him, causing hellish pain with each cry and movement. He found that even these powerful earth-bound spirits were bound to the Dreaming Laws and as they wept inconsolably for that chance lost, their anger increased. They began to weave parts of skin and hair from his physical body into a *mask of cessation*, they called it, as they placed it over his eyes and mouth. "As such pain you wished to give, man of dust, so it shall be for you," they mumbled and murmured among themselves. Then, while he was yet alive and helpless, they began to peel skin from his body. Eerwa tried to scream out his pain but the mask held every cry inside him and over his muffled screams, he could still hear their mocking words of warning.

"After a time and more time, ignorant son of dust, your pain will end," they raged at him as they tore at his skin. "Next, you will meet the Great Spirit and reap the consequences of your selfish wants," they mocked. "*How* you will pay for the dreadful debasements performed on your own people," they cried, as he screamed silently through waves of bright rolling pain. But the old spirits chuckled and giggled through his pain, deriding his hard-fought for powers while continuing his edification, even as they stripped him skinless. "Once there," they told him, relentlessly carrying out their work, "you will await spiritual judgment, skinless and in pain, before being released back into the world as some part of the whole again; oh Great Death-adder," the teasing voices said, laughing wildly at his cries, which only slowed then became silent as he died physically, only to find his spirit trapped there with the same scornful, howling old ones that he'd wished to exploit. Even that terrible scream of pure anguish was forced back inside his tormented spirit by the mask they'd created from his own body.

As his besieged spirit left his tormented body, Nyarla – her work done – began to move across the land toward the camp of the clan who had called her here. Then for some unfathomed reason, she remembered a moment many years ago, when her then mentor, Kulardja Sky-stone, had suggested to her that evil spirits came back as inanimate objects, forced to watch the people on the land go about their lives for many, many moons, until the price of their crimes had been paid in full. She wondered if she would recognise the sorcerer's spirit, bound to a rock or similar object. She knew stranger things had happened. There'd been one old gnarled tree that never grew leaves, but stayed alive for generations and was said to hold the spirit of one such dark-spirited sorcerer in punishment. Trainee warriors had used that old tree for spear and boomerang practice for as long as she could remember and the gum resin that flowed from its wounds was thick and red and even smelled like old blood. As she moved across the cool desert sand, Nyarla could feel that the sorcerer's tortured spirit had not been allowed to leave as yet and she shivered a little and began to move faster, wanting to feel the warmth of live human spirits around her again …

CHAPTER 4

THE MESSENGER'S CAMP

Back at Buryldanji's home fire, a quiet sense of expectancy had taken over the camp. After the massive play of light and colour in the sky the previous night and several sightings of the clan's sacred dingo spirit being reported that morning, his people were on edge. Then, at false dawn, the elder who'd sent Buryldanji to the Fethafoot had been spotted watching and waiting for someone from a small hilltop close to camp. Now, the whole tribe seemed to hold its breath in anticipation of some major event, creating an unusual silence that kept even the suckling children quiet on this morning. As Buryldanji washed himself and steeped his smouldering fire, he noticed the elder's gaze turn to a well-worn track that the clan's children used when searching for tucker, near the base of a set of scrub covered hills. Then his worried face broke into a huge welcoming smile as he recognised Nyarla stepping up, head bowed, to greet the elder at his waiting place.

The old man sat quietly in the cool of the morning, gazing away from Nyarla. He sat still, looking around anywhere but at the young woman, in the correct manner, until enough time had passed to allow her to indicate her respect. When he spoke, it was to ask after her mother and grandmother. After another short silence, while he worked out her lineage, he frowned, his confusion evident, then he looked into her dark brown eyes intently for a few long moments. Suddenly, his old eyes opened wider and though he tried not to show his surprise, his aged body changed posture abruptly, whispering his knowledge of her power and humbly held authority. When he looked into her eyes again and she nodded slightly at him, he knew that the bad spirit was gone and would trouble them no more.

The elder sat quietly again for several minutes, gathering his shocked sense of dignity to him before he spoke again. Nyarla meanwhile remained silent, her gaze averted as custom requested and allowing the elder to gather the questions that she'd guessed he might ask. This old fellow however, was wise, dignified and a man of few words. His proficient wisdom and insight informed him that he was in the presence of a Fethafoot adept. Never mind her youth or gender, he was old and wise enough to look beyond her appearance and spot the tell-tale signs of power and training. Instead of boring her with a lot of questions, he smiled at her and nodded once, surprising her, as he waited on her answers to questions that he'd not yet uttered.

Nyarla then understood that he would not ask for specifics about the bad spirit, or its end. She knew the important aspect for him now was to submit the victims' bodies back to the Dreaming. After that grief-stricken custom was completed, normal activities like ceremonial routine, initiations and maintaining their physical piece of the Dreaming – their own land and clan Dreaming paths – could go on as was proper. The elder's first actual words to Nyarla revealed some of this elder's raw power, as if he had read even her guarded mind as he explained his people's situation. "Even maintenance of the few local waterholes, sacred places for our full tribe has stopped, with the terror never letting up; a thing unheard of, before its coming," he said to her softly.

"We are indebted to your family," he spoke again, with the seriousness of acknowledging such a weighty obligation in his old voice. The elder continued, again revealing a great intelligence and awareness of the large country that the Fethafoot family watched over. "I also understand your family's use of reputation amongst our people, all across Heart-rock, " he told her and now, his lined and weathered old black face crinkled into a small boy's cheeky smile, as he continued. "Hear and understand me warrior, my circle of peers will ensure a great and noble story, of how the Terror of our country was cut down by a worse and much more capable terror; a lone Fethafoot!" he said, and his rheumy old eyes sparkled and smiled gratefully. Nyarla raised her own keen curious eyes to the elder and began to explain what she knew was necessary, rather than any precise detail of her actions.

"Wise elder," the young warrior began, while glancing at the many wonderful lines and scars that were so much a part of the secure gentleness that she felt in this powerful, wise old man. "I backtracked the shameless one after the Judging and found the remains of the missing in The Mother's blood tunnels; that smooth-walled, underground cave and tunnel system there," she said, chin-lipping in its direction. She didn't bother to tell him that she had asked for help from the mother eagle again, when even her faultless eyes lost the tiny traces Eerwa had left, as he used all his great skill to evade sight or capture. She had taken bearings from local landmarks and knew that the local tribe would have no problem locating the place where the bodies lay. But Nyarla could also sense that this old clever-man was still personally curious to know how such a small, innocent looking young woman, could overcome and kill such a demented and seemingly strong evil spirit, despite his own years of experience in hiding his thoughts.

Thinking about the need for her family's mysterious reputation to be supported, though personally despising boasting as such and with a slight twinkle in her eyes, Nyarla finally spoke sparingly about the Terror's end. "I know that you understand how it sits, grand-father elder," she said, giving the most worthy personal compliment she could to the astute elder.

"Most shameless ones are so full of themselves that they often underestimate people, who in their distorted view, are of little or no importance," she explained simply.

"The Terror's remains lie out in the ancient circle of stones – the place of many deaths." She gestured toward the tribe's well-known and sacred area, which only a man as powerful as this old man could go to and return without harm.

Then, with a short, chopping wave of her hand downward, an innocent smile and respectful nod – all subtle actions stating that her clan work was done, she squat and rested her back against a nearby tree. Nyarla knew that to tell little was the clever thing to do, as the old man would embellish on the details in his own way and with broad, oral brush strokes, in the best tradition of all great storytellers: especially after he went to burn the evil thing's remains and saw its torn, wretched state.

Having thanked the elder for hearing her and now having concluded her clan business, Nyarla left him there and went to visit Buryldanji and to say goodbye. She would not stay for the many ceremonies that would accompany the removal of the bodies from the cave, nor the preparations for the spirits to travel, as she was not from this area and it would be disrespectful, as she had no kin here at all. She would travel to the drier lands of the Pitta-Pitta people, where she would rest, regather her strength and meditate in the true clear desert plains, just south from what is now the mining city of Mt Isa. She would use her time there to rest and to clear her spirit after taking human life. There, she would also hear from her family and would either go back to join them, or possibly be sent on to another family mission, somewhere in her beloved great country …

The oldest human story

Poor love-struck Buryldanji, now even more admiring of this capable young woman that the whole tribe had been whispering about, felt an aching pain and loss; a feeling unknown to him before their meeting and journey across Heart-rock.

The young man had been in a type of passionate fever ever since the first few days' travel with Nyarla and had hoped against hope to see more of her and spend more time together before she left – and here, she had come to him. They were silent as they walked together, placidly this time, to the edges of his lands. Nyarla, being a flesh and blood young woman as well as a Fethafoot, felt his love and pain and in no great hurry to be on her own again as she would be for most of her journey, she requested him again to rest and lay with her this night.

Thus, evening found them camped again in simple luxury on the banks of a small inland lake: a life-giving inland watercourse, abundant with wildlife and native vegetation. The lake was filled with clear clean freshwater, which was filtered clear and sweet by the surrounding sands it ran through. Fethafoot history said this lake was created in the Dreamtime, as a place so beautiful that the Rainbow Serpent himself would rest there as he gave shape and form to the land. The only hint left to its ancient beauty it is said – was the name itself, which had remained through time and even in the oldest Ghost language translated to: "love of God". Today however, this once glorious ancient place is the searing dry salt flats of Lake Amadeus.

As night fell and with the magnificent colours and sounds of the Australian desert evening accompanying the eager couple, they loved again. They loved each other, the land, The Great Spirit and the Dreaming that brought them together. The world's many great poets and famous painters, renowned writers and wisest philosophers would struggle to capture the warm salty essence of *this* earthy joining: two dark and dusty, naked, sinuously glistening humans did what we have done for millennia. Together, Nyarla and Buryldanji's raw youthful passion swept aside all other cares as they unbound the withheld desires of spirit and flesh, becoming as one for those few short minutes that all humans need: riding the wave of life together, perchance to dally in spirit together for a pure moment. The young early Australians stiffened, they softened and sighed, they cried and growled as they touched and were touched under the watching wide night sky …

The circle of stones
It was that same clear sweet roof of air dew, stars and moon that equally gave ethereal visage to a lone body lying still now finally, in a circle of stones not so distant from the hungry animated lovers. Eerwa's once greedy shameless eyes, dusted with sand and sightless, lay open to the same view that our Fethafoot warrior and her lover rose toward together. Both young lovers yearning to break out from the flesh and to meet in spirit, in their inescapable quest for the release and spending and

gathering of seed. That instinctive need for survival of their people – giving all to each other and once more, creating the possibility of life and the unadulterated power of continued existence: simply from giving to one another in the earthy passion, aptly experienced by the language creatures as *love* ...

THE END

Like this story? Read on with

The
FETHAFOOT CHRONICLES
BOOK 2

GULUYA
and the
LAKE MUNGO MYSTERY

AUSTRALIA, AROUND 39,987BP
(BEFORE THE PRESENT)

This chronicle comes alive from the legend of a great sweeping saga, which covered the lives of four Australians who lived and died numerous generations ago. Their meeting and lives together left an archaeological puzzle that stands even today. In those times, our chronicle reveals, Mega-fauna, the giant-sized animal ancestors of our modern day fauna still roamed across our lands.

The stage is set, the lights drop, the curtain rises – and when the lights come back up at the scene of a 'dig' on the shores of Lake Mungo, two Australian archaeologists have just uncovered two sets of ancient bones.

ABOUT THE AUTHOR

Pemulwuy Weeatunga is the pen name John M Wenitong chose for the *Fethafoot Chronicles* series.

Born in Gladstone, Queensland, Australia, John is an indigenous Australian man of Kabi Kabi Aboriginal and South-Sea Island origin. His Australian indigenous mob is caretakers of the mainland area from approximately the Fraser to Moreton Islands area of the SE-Queensland coastline.

John's mother – Aunty Lorna Wenitong – started the first Aboriginal Health Program out of Mt Isa in the late 1960s and his younger brother, Mark, one of the first indigenous Doctors in Queensland, is credited with being the mind behind AIDA in Australia.

John, now in his early sixties, has four children aged from their teens to their late thirties, and six wonderful grandchildren. He plays guitar, photographs nature, writes poetry and songs, and occasionally tries to sing.

http://thefethafootchronicles.com.au

Lightning Source UK Ltd.
Milton Keynes UK
UKHW011509260320
360870UK00014B/245

The
FETHAFOOT CHRONICLES
BOOK 1

NYARLA
and the
CIRCLE OF STONES

Pemulwuy Weeatunga

This is an IndieMosh book
brought to you by MoshPit Publishing
an imprint of Mosher's Business Support Pty Ltd
PO BOX 147
Hazelbrook NSW 2779
www.indiemosh.com.au

First published 2015 © Pemulwuy Weeatunga

Cataloguing-in-Publication entry is available from the National Library of Australia: http://catalogue.nla.gov.au/

Title:	Nyarla and the Circle of Stones
Series:	The Fethafoot Chronicles
Volume:	Book 1
Author:	Weeatunga, Pemulwuy
ISBNs:	978-1-925595-99-4 (paperback)

Cover design: John M Wenitong